GUINEA PIGS ONLINE

BUNNY TROUBLE

'EGG-CELLENT!'
Micespace.com

JENNIFER GRAY &
AMANDA SWIFT

GUINEA PIGS ONLINE BUNNY TROUBLE

Jennifer Gray & Amanda Swift

Illustrations by Sarah Horne

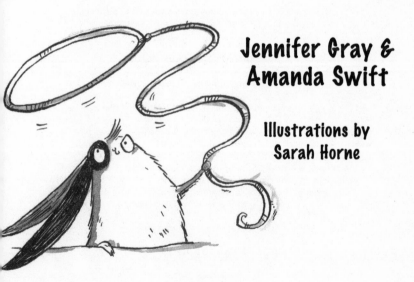

Quercus

New York • London

Quercus

New York • London

© 2014 by Jennifer Gray and Amanda Swift
Illustrations © 2014 by Sarah Horne

First published in the United States by Quercus in 2015

ISBN 978-1-62365-947-9

Library of Congress Control Number: 2015930240

Distributed in the United States and Canada by
Hachette Book Group
1290 Avenue of the Americas
New York, NY 10104

Manufactured in the United States

2 4 6 8 10 9 7 5 3 1

www.quercus.com

Contents

1
Binny

It was springtime and at number 7
Middleton Crescent, the guinea pigs
were doing their spring cleaning.
Outside the sun was shining, the
birds were singing, the trees were
turning green and the flowers were
humming with bees. It was the right

time of year to make everything
spick and span.

Fuzzy and Coco were listening to
their favorite radio station, Animals
Extra, while they tidied up the hutch.
Fuzzy jiggled in time to the music
as he put the bits of cereal that had
fallen out of his bowl back into it.
Coco hummed along as she pushed
the nice, fresh hay into one corner and
arranged her hairbrushes and
bows in neat rows.

Then Fuzzy organized all the vegetables they were going to eat for their supper. He put the cabbage leaves in one pile, the sweet spring carrots in another pile, the broccoli stalks in a third pile, and he ate the last bit of watercress because he couldn't think what else to do with it.

"Those vegetables look delicious, Fuzzy," said Coco. She scuttled over. "I'm starving! Do you think we can have a break now?" Tidying up was hard work. She was glad they only did it in the spring. The rest of the time their owners, Ben and Henrietta, tidied up for them.

Fuzzy looked around the hutch. It was perfect. Even their poo tray was tidy.

"Yes, let's take a break," he said. "I tell you what, why don't we see if we can find Eduardo?"

Eduardo was Fuzzy and Coco's friend who lived at the bottom of the garden in the copse. Ben and Henrietta didn't know that the guinea pigs could let themselves out of their hutch and wriggle through the old cat flap into the back garden whenever they wanted to see their friends.

"Good idea!" said Coco. She wondered which bow to wear. Something pretty, she thought, for spring. Yellow, maybe—the color of daffodils.

She was just tying the yellow bow when the news came on the radio:

"This is Animal Extra News. We have just heard that the Strawberry Park Animal Rescue Center is to close . . ."

Coco stopped tying her yellow bow. Fuzzy stopped trying out his dance moves. They both listened carefully. The animal rescue center was where their owner Ben worked.

"Reports suggest that all the animal cages need replacing, but the center does not have enough money to cover the cost. Peggy from Pets2Go, the pet shop next door, has taken in all the animals until homes can be found for them. Ben Bliss, who runs the rescue center, has said that he

will have to cancel the popular Easter Fair.
It is believed the center will be sold."

Coco started to cry, and even
Fuzzy had a tear in his eye. The Easter
Fair was the best thing about Easter!
The rescue center was decorated with
yellow balloons and spring flowers and
open to visitors all day. There was
music, chocolate, and games. Lots of
animals were adopted and went off to
live in nice homes for the rest of their
lives. And the fair was due to take
place in only four days' time.

Just then, the guinea-pig friends
heard the front door bang. It was

followed by the sound of sobbing. Someone blew their nose loudly.

"It's Ben," Fuzzy whispered.

The guinea pigs listened as Ben's footsteps went down the stairs to the kitchen.

They peeped out through the wire of the hutch.

Ben was covered in sawdust. His clothes were very, very dirty and his eyes were red from crying. He went over to the fruit bowl. Fuzzy and Coco watched as Ben took some of his favorite big green grapes and went back into the hall. This was very

9

unlike him. He usually came over to say hello to Fuzzy and Coco first.

"Poor Ben," Coco whispered. "He must be terribly upset about the rescue center closing."

"I wish there was something we could do!" Fuzzy sighed.

SCRATCH! SCRATCH! SCRATCH!

"What's that noise?" Coco asked.

It was coming from the hallway, where Ben had gone.

Just then Ben came back into the kitchen carrying a cage with three big padlocks on it. The corners of the cage bristled with extra screws. It tipped from side to side in his arms.

SCRATCH! SCRATCH! SCRATCH!

The noise was coming from inside the cage. Whatever was inside seemed very keen to get out.

"Stop struggling!" Ben said, trying to keep the cage level.

CRASH!

"What was that?" said Coco. The crashing sound had come from above them.

"Ben's put that cage on the roof of our hutch!" Fuzzy squeaked.

The hutch rocked.

"That's it!" said Ben angrily. "I've had enough! You've made a total mess of the rescue center! You've chewed through all the cages, just when I was trying to get everything ready for the Easter Fair. It's thanks to you it's got to close. You're staying here until you've learned how to behave! Then we'll find you a new home."

"It must be one of the animals from the rescue center," Fuzzy whispered.

"Why does it have to come here?" Coco complained. "I mean, it said on the news that the animals had gone to Peggy at Pets2Go." She didn't like the idea of having to share Ben and Henrietta with another animal. She liked things at number 7 Middleton Crescent just the way they were.

"Don't be like that, Coco," Fuzzy

said. "It's only going to be here for a little while—until Ben finds it a new home."

"But we don't even know what sort of animal it is!" Coco squeaked. Ben handled all kinds of animals at the rescue center.

"Just try to be good," Ben said with a sigh. "No more chewing. Or burping. Or farting. I'll be back in a little while, when I've showered off the sawdust. Don't go away." He disappeared back upstairs.

THUMP, THUMP, THUMP.

The guinea pigs glanced upward.

This new noise was coming from the cage.

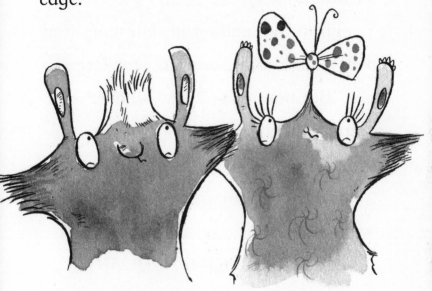

THUMP, THUMP, THUMP.

Coco nudged Fuzzy. "Go have a look."

"No way," said Fuzzy. "I'm not

having a look until I know what sort of animal it is."

From the amount of thumping that was going on, it sounded very large.

"But you won't know what it is until you have a look."

"But—"

They were interrupted by another sound.

CHOMP, CHOMP, CHOMP.

CHOMP, CHOMP, CHOMP.

Fuzzy gulped. "Whatever it is, it's definitely hungry!"

Coco began to tremble. "It couldn't be Renard, could it?"

Renard was the evil fox who lived in the copse.

"I don't think so," Fuzzy replied. "Ben would never bring him home to live with us."

CHOMP, CHOMP, CHOMP.

The eating continued. It got louder and louder. It got nearer and nearer. And then there was a crack in the wooden roof of Coco and Fuzzy's hutch, then another crack, and then cracks everywhere. And then the roof crashed to the floor.

Fuzzy and Coco clutched each other in terror!

Then, to their surprise, the cutest, fluffiest little baby bunny they had ever seen landed in the hutch. She was white all over with black ears and big eyes.

The baby bunny looked around her. She looked at Coco and Fuzzy, who were still gazing at her in astonishment. She looked at the tidy hutch and at the pile of hay in the corner and at the clean poo tray. Then she hopped over to the neat piles of vegetables Fuzzy had arranged for the guinea pigs' supper. She munched the tastiest cabbage leaf, turned around and then she did a big poo on top of the rest of the food.

PLOP! PLOP! PLOP!
PLOP! PLOP! PLOP!

When she'd finished, she turned to Fuzzy and Coco.

"Hi there," she said. "I'm Binny!"

2
grounded

The next day, at the bottom of the garden, Fuzzy and Coco told the whole terrible story to their friends. Eduardo was there, and so were Banoffee, Banoffee's oldest son, Terry, and her thirteen other children.

"It was Binny who caused all the

damage at the rescue center," Fuzzy said. "It's because of her that it has to close down. Binny chewed through all the cages and Ben doesn't have the money to replace them. He says it's a total mess."

"That's why Peggy from Pets2Go didn't take Binny in with the rest of the animals," said Coco. "I don't blame her!"

"But how did she get into your hutch?" Terry asked.

"She chewed through the floor of her cage," Coco said. "Then she chewed through our roof."

"*Caramba*, that bunny must have teeth like a chinchilla!" Eduardo said solemnly. "They can chew through anything!"

"What's a chinchilla?" Blossom, Banoffee's youngest baby, asked.

"It is a big Peruvian *squirl*," Eduardo explained.

"Squirrel," Coco corrected him. Eduardo was from Peru. He had traveled all the way from Peru to free the guinea pigs of the world, only he'd gotten a bit lost and ended up in Strawberry Park by mistake. He'd also been very disappointed to find that most of the guinea pigs he met there didn't want to be free. They wanted to be pets, like Fuzzy and Coco.

"We've told you before, Eduardo, it's a squirrel, not a *squirl*." Coco could be quite bossy sometimes without

24

really meaning it. Especially when she was around Eduardo, whom she secretly liked.

Eduardo frowned.

"Never mind Binny," Fuzzy said. "The point is, what are we going to do to save the rescue center?"

"There's nothing we can do, Fuzzy," Coco told him.

"There must be something." Fuzzy scratched his crest. "I know—we could make a website asking people to help clear up the rescue center and fix the cages. Maybe then we can have the Easter Fair after all."

"I'll help you, Fuzzy," Terry said. "I know what to do."

Fuzzy and Terry both loved computers.

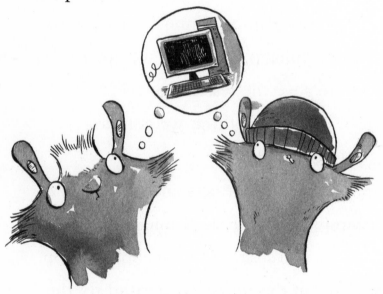

"Good." Coco had been listening to the conversation impatiently.

"Now we've gotten that out of the way, let's get back to Binny. We've got to get rid of her."

"But you said she's only a baby," Banoffee protested. "You can't get rid of her."

"I don't care. She's got to go."

"Why don't we try and teach her how to behave?" Fuzzy suggested. "Then if my website works she can still be adopted at the Easter Fair."

"The Easter Fair!" Blossom cried. "Will there be chocolate eggs?"

"Chocolate! Chocolate!" Banoffee's children chanted. They had heard of

chocolate, but they had never had any.
That didn't stop them wanting some,
though.

"We want chocolate!" they yelled.

"Pah!" Eduardo said angrily.

"Guinea pigs don't eat chocolate. They should be foraging for chickweed in the wild. In fact, they shouldn't be in a rescue center at all. Or a pet shop. They should be free!"

A thought struck him. He wriggled his bushy eyebrows. "THAT'S IT, *amigos*!" he cried. "This bunny the binny—she is a freedom fighter like me! She wishes to join her brothers in the wild and sing songs around the camp fire."

"It's *Binny* the *bunny* and it doesn't sound like she's a freedom fighter to me." Terry scratched his wool hat. "Sounds more like she's bored."

"Bored?" Fuzzy repeated.

"Yeah, like she doesn't have enough to do," Terry explained. "I used to be a bit like that, didn't I, Mom, when I was a teen-pig?"

"You were!" Banoffee agreed. "You were awful before you got into computers. You used to sit around watching TV all day."

"So you think if we keep Binny busy, she'll stop chewing our hutch

31

and pooing in our food?" Coco asked.

"Bound to," said Terry.

"Well, that's settled then," Coco said quickly. She'd had an idea: one that involved her showing off, which was always the best kind of idea as far as Coco was concerned. "Fuzzy and Terry, you can teach her how to use the computer. Banoffee, you can show her how to do her hair nicely . . ."

Banoffee clapped her paws together happily. She loved doing hair.

"And I," Coco said grandly, "will teach her Good Manners. I learned

them from the Queen," she added,
in case anyone had forgotten. "One
used to live at Buckingham Palace,
you know."

Eduardo sniggered.

"What's so funny about that?"
Coco demanded.

"You pet guinea pigs crack me
up!" he scoffed. "Computers, hairstyles
and good manners? Are you kidding
me? What that binny needs is some
fresh air."

He scuttled off under the gate into
the copse. Then, when no one called
after him, he poked his head back

through and shouted, "Just you wait
and see."

When they returned to the house,
Binny was busy chewing her way
through a chair leg. Ben had tried to
patch up her cage with another piece
of wood and some more screws the

night before, but he had given up when Binny chewed her way through that as well. Before they went out, Ben and Henrietta had left Binny in the kitchen with some newspaper in the corner for her to poo on.

"Look at that!" Coco said in disgust.

Binny had pooed everywhere except on the newspaper.

"Come along!" Coco picked her way through the droppings toward the clean newspaper.

She was followed by Banoffee and all of Banoffee's children, except Terry. Banoffee had agreed that they should join in the lesson on good manners because sometimes they forgot to use a tissue when they had a runny nose. And all the grown-up guinea pigs (apart from Eduardo of course) agreed it was more likely that Binny would behave if she was part of a group.

"Make two rows," Coco ordered. "And leave a space in the middle at the front for Binny."

Binny looked up from chewing the chair leg when she heard her name.

The guinea piglets did as they were told. They made two rows, with space between Blossom and Pepper, Banoffee's second youngest, at the front.

"Come and sit down, Binny," Coco said.

Binny put her head to one side. Her ears waggled. "Say, 'Please,'" she said. "It's good manners."

Coco blushed. The guinea piglets stared at her, wide-eyed. Then they stared at Binny.

"Come and sit down, Binny, PLEASE!" Coco said with exaggerated politeness.

"No THANKS," Binny said.

Some of the guinea piglets started to giggle.

Coco frowned. "I can't teach you good manners if you won't sit down, Binny," she said.

"So what?" Binny said rudely.

Suddenly she burped.

"Say, 'Excuse me!'" Coco ordered.

"Excuse you!" Binny said.

The guinea piglets all laughed.

Coco was horrified. They were laughing at her!

PLOP! PLOP! PLOP! Suddenly Binny let out a volley of droppings.

"Binny!" Coco squealed. "Use the newspaper! That's what it's there for."

Binny thought about this for a moment. "OK," she agreed.

PLOP. PLOP. PLOP. PLOP. PLOP. PLOP. Before Coco realized what was happening, Binny shot across the room and started pooing all around the guinea piglets.

"My babies!" Banoffee shrieked.

Coco hid under a cushion.

The guinea piglets were covered in rabbit poo. It was all over their beautiful hairstyles.

"It'll take me days to get this out!"

Banoffee sobbed. She gathered her children up and shooed them out of the cat flap.

PLOP! PLOP! PLOP! PLOP! PLOP! PLOP!

Coco peeped out from under the cushion. She was surrounded by a sea of poo.

"Fuzzy, do something!" she begged.

"Binny, how about you learn to use the computer?" Fuzzy suggested.

"OK," Binny agreed reluctantly, "but I thought you wanted me to use the newspaper." She hopped over.

"*NO!*" Fuzzy and Terry closed the

lid of Ben's laptop just in time to stop
Binny from pooing on that as well.

Just then they heard Ben's key in
the latch.

"I'm out of here." Terry raced after
his brothers and sisters. "Good luck!"
He wriggled out of the cat flap.

Fuzzy and Coco rushed back to their hutch. Ben and Henrietta couldn't find out they'd escaped, or they'd put a new lock on the hutch door.

They heard Ben's footsteps on the stairs.

He opened the kitchen door.

"Yuk!" he said. The guinea pigs watched as he got out a dustpan and brush and swept up all the droppings into the trash.

"Binny!" he called. "Binny!" She scampered over to him. Ben reached out his hand to her. To the guinea pigs' surprise, rather than biting his

finger, she allowed
him to scratch her
gently between the
ears. "Good girl,"
Ben said. "That's
much better."

"Good girl!"
Coco squealed to Fuzzy. "Good girl?"

Coco's chattering attracted Ben's
attention. Of course he didn't know
that the guinea pigs were talking to
each other, because although guinea
pigs can understand humans, humans
can't understand guinea pigs. But he did
understand that Coco sounded upset.

Ben walked over to the cage with a smile and put his face to the wire.

"There's no need to be jealous," he said kindly.

Then he stopped smiling. Instead his face wore a big frown.

He pulled out his cell phone and dialed a number.

"Henrietta," he said into the phone, "you'd better come and see this."

"What is it?" Henrietta's voice sounded worried.

"It's Coco and Fuzzy," Ben said. "They must have gotten out."

Coco and Fuzzy glanced at each other. How did he know?

"And they've done something terrible." Ben burst into tears.

Terrible? What did he mean? They hadn't done anything!

"They've eaten my favorite grapes!" Ben sniveled.

The guinea pigs glanced behind them. Sure enough a forest of grape stalks and a few pips littered the hutch.

"Binny!" Fuzzy and Coco sighed.

3
Save the Rescue Center

Ben and Henrietta knew a lot about pets. They knew that they couldn't let a naughty event like stealing Ben's favorite grapes go unpunished, in case it happened again. They took away Fuzzy and Coco's sweet spring carrots so that they would learn a lesson about not stealing other people's food. Of course what they didn't know was that Coco and Fuzzy weren't naughty at all. It was Binny who had stolen and eaten the grapes, but she had made it look as if Coco and Fuzzy had done it!

Coco and Fuzzy sat in their hutch feeling sad. They couldn't even go out in the garden because, just as they had feared, Ben had put a new lock on the hutch and they couldn't figure out how to open it. Luckily Eduardo popped into the kitchen through the old cat flap to see where they were.

"*Amigos!*" he exclaimed. "Why are you not outside in the beautiful sunshine?"

Fuzzy nodded toward the door of the hutch. Eduardo gasped when he saw the new lock.

"But how did this happen?"

Fuzzy told him. When he got to the part about the manners lesson and the poo problem, Eduardo laughed.

"It's not funny," Coco said angrily. "Imagine if the Queen had been there."

"Anyway, then Ben came home," Fuzzy continued, "and discovered the grape stalks in *our* hutch. He thought we'd gotten out and stolen his favorite grapes. That's why he grounded us and put the new lock on. I mean, we did get out, obviously, but we didn't steal the grapes. It was Binny."

"Hmmm." Eduardo pondered for a moment. "Well, you are in luck, *amigos*. For I, Eduardo Julio Antonio del Monte, will free you." He got his skeleton keys out of his satchel. They were keys that could open any lock.

Eduardo always carried them, just in case he got trapped somewhere and needed to escape back to freedom in a hurry. Carefully he placed a skeleton key in the lock and twisted it gently in his paws.

PING!

The lock sprang open.

"You should have asked me to rescue you this morning," Eduardo said to the friends as they trotted out of the hutch. "I didn't have nothing to do except write freedom songs."

"How could we ask you when we were locked in the hutch?" said Coco grumpily. She hadn't enjoyed sitting in there with a load of grape stalks and no spring carrots to eat.

"Well, come now into the garden," said Eduardo, pointing to the cat flap, "and I'll sing my new song to you!"

"No thanks, Eduardo," Fuzzy said. "I need to make my website. And I still haven't tried to teach Binny how to use the computer. I really think that might work. I don't know any young creature who doesn't like learning online."

"You can try," Eduardo said,

shrugging, "and when it doesn't work out, you can send her into the garden to learn with me. You coming, Coco?"

"No thank you," said Coco. "I'll come out when we've finished with Binny."

"See you in two minutes then," said Eduardo as he hopped out of the cat flap.

"Ha ha!" Coco called after him. She really hoped Fuzzy was right about teaching Binny to use the computer: at least it would shut Eduardo up.

Although Binny was naughty most of the time, she was also still very young so she spent the rest of the time asleep. She was snoozing in the corner of her hutch when Fuzzy tapped on the chewed wire.

"Binny," he called, "do you want to see some nice bunnies?"

Binny opened one eye.

"I've been dreaming about grapes," she yawned.

"Good for you," said Coco sourly. "I've been having nightmares about them."

Binny chewed a hole in the wire and jumped out. "Where are these bunnies, then?" she said, looking around the room.

"They're not real bunnies," said Fuzzy. "They're on the computer."

Henrietta had taken the laptop to work so the guinea pigs had to use the big computer on the table.

"How are we going to get up there?" Binny asked. Like most guinea pigs, rabbits can't climb.

"Like this!" Coco and Fuzzy showed Binny how to use "the jump." The jump was a clever device that the guinea pigs used to get up on things such as tables and computer desks when their owners weren't around. It worked like a seesaw with a flat part (in this case a ruler) balanced over a triangular part (in this case a bit of chair leg Binny had chewed off).

Coco and Fuzzy balanced the ruler on the chewed chair leg.

"Sit on that end," Fuzzy told Binny.

Binny hopped on to one end of the ruler and sat down.

"Here goes!" Fuzzy took a running jump and landed on the other end.

"Wheeee!" Binny looked like she enjoyed being catapulted into the air and giggled when she landed on the table.

Coco
realized that
she'd never heard
Binny giggle before.
Maybe as well as being a naughty
bunny, she wasn't always a very
happy bunny?

It was Fuzzy's turn next. He
landed beside Binny on the table.

"What about her?" Binny asked,
pointing at Coco.

"You should call me 'Coco,' not 'her'!" Coco said. "And it's rude to point." She wriggled up the wire at the back of the computer. "One learned to climb when one was at Buckingham Palace, playing the harp," she explained.

Binny looked at her blankly.

"You can find anything you want on the computer," said Fuzzy, turning it on. "What would you like to look at?"

"Home," said Binny right away.

"Well, I guess home for you is the rescue center."

Fuzzy found the Strawberry Park
Animal Rescue Center website.

"There you are!" said Fuzzy,
flicking through photos of rabbits
being adopted by loving children.

Binny suddenly burst into tears. Not just a few little drips but great big gulpy sobs.

"Whatever's the matter?" asked Coco, who hated seeing anyone cry, even a naughty bunny like Binny.

"I—I—I—want to go home," wailed Binny.

"To the rescue center?" asked Fuzzy.

"No, to a real home!" she sniffed.

Fuzzy tried to cheer Binny up by clicking on a photo of last year's Easter Fair.

"Look, Binny. That's the Easter

Fair. It happens every year. Lots of children come and all the animals get adopted. That could happen to you on Saturday. If my website works."

"But I chewed through the cages," Binny said. "The rescue center's finished. Ben said so."

"Not necessarily," Fuzzy said. "We're going to try to save it by asking people on the computer to help fix the cages and clean up." He tapped the keyboard.

"What are you doing?" Binny asked.

"I'm making a website with a
photograph of you I've taken from the
rescue center homepage. See?"

MICESPACE

STRAWBERRY PARK RESCUE CENTRE

*Urgent! Help fix cages and spring clean
the rescue center on Saturday in time
for the Easter Fair. Good homes needed for
Binny the Easter Bunny and other animals.*

 Join

Comment

Binny pointed to the bottom of the page. "What does that part mean?"

"If people want to help," Fuzzy explained, "they click on the box. That way we know how many people will be coming. And they can leave a comment if they want to."

"And what's the Easter Bunny?" asked Binny, reading the screen carefully.

"It's a bunny that brings happiness at Easter."

"And chocolate," said Coco, remembering the tiny piece of chocolate egg she'd had last year.

"There," said Fuzzy. "The website has gone live."

"Was it dead?" asked Binny.

"No, I mean anyone who has the Internet can look at it now," Fuzzy explained.

"Thank you," said Binny, and then she burst into tears again.

"What's the matter now?" asked Coco.

"I'm not good!" wailed Binny. "So no one will want me!"

"You *will* be good," said Coco, "by next week. And then everyone will want you."

Binny's face brightened. She looked much happier. Coco didn't look quite so happy. This was because she didn't believe what she'd just said. Even if the Easter Fair went ahead, Binny would never be ready. She and Fuzzy had tried everything they could. Unless . . .

Coco sighed. There was only one thing for it.

They would have to ask Eduardo for help.

4
Eduardo Takes Charge

"I'm Binny the bunny,
I live in the copse,
I'm here to fight for freedom
And biff Renard the fox.

Eduardo is my hero,
He's cool and strong and brave,

He'll teach me to light fires
And dig my own cave!"

"Excellent!" Eduardo applauded. "That's the spirit, Bunny! Well done! I especially like the first two lines of the second verse."

It was the next day and the animals were in the garden. Eduardo had arrived just after lunch to let Fuzzy and Coco out of the hutch and to collect Binny. His first lesson for Binny was to write a freedom song.

Binny thumped her foot on the ground happily.

Coco and Fuzzy looked on. "Are you sure this is a good idea?" Coco whispered.

Fuzzy looked at her in astonishment. "It was your idea, Coco!" he reminded her. "You were the one who said we should let Eduardo try to help Binny."

"Oh yes." Coco could be a bit

forgetful. "Well, at least she seems to be enjoying herself."

Pleased with the success of her freedom song, Binny was racing around the garden, stopping occasionally to chew Ben and Henrietta's best plants.

"Maybe Eduardo was right," Coco added. It was hard for her to say this because she didn't usually like it when Eduardo was right. But on this occasion, if it was good for Binny, she didn't mind.

Fuzzy squeezed her paw.

"Cooee!" It was Banoffee. She

appeared through the hole in the garden fence.

"The kids are all ready," she told Eduardo. "Except Terry, who doesn't really like outdoor games."

"Ready for what?" Fuzzy asked.

"Eduardo's offered to take them on a camping trip!" Banoffee explained. "Just for the afternoon," she added. "They need to be home for supper."

"Banoffee!" Eduardo said sternly. "I have already told you. They will not need supper. They will forage for food in the copse."

"OK, well, it's there if they want it," Banoffee said. "Come on, kids."

Banoffee's children popped through the fence, one by one. Some of them held sticks. Others had hats. Pepper was carrying a basket.

"What's that for?" Coco asked.

"To put things in," Pepper said promptly. "When we go foraging."

"Good thinking." Eduardo clapped. "Now listen, everyone. First up, it is very important not to get lost in the wild. *Get lost, get eaten*, that's what I was taught. So you must each have a partner. Binny, you go with Blossom. The rest of you make pairs."

The children did as they were told. Even Binny.

"This seems to be working really well!" Fuzzy remarked.

"I told you so!" Eduardo said.

He was bragging! Coco reminded herself not to get upset.

"OK, let's go." Eduardo led the procession under the fence at the bottom of the garden into the copse.

Coco and Fuzzy followed a little way behind while Banoffee went back to her hutch to make the supper, just in case.

The copse was a patch of wild ground with long grass, some dense bushes and a big oak tree in the middle of a clearing. Eduardo's burrow was under the oak tree in a hollowed-out den among the tree roots.

Eduardo marched the guinea piglets briskly through the grass. He stopped at the clearing, beside the entrance to his burrow.

"What about Renard?" Coco said nervously, glancing around. The fox had once sneaked up on her under the oak tree and tried to eat her. She didn't want him doing that to Banoffee's children or Binny.

"Yeah, let's get him!" Binny cried.

Eduardo frowned. "Bunny," he said, "do not speak no more about that. You need to be an expert in freedom fighting like me before you can fight Renard."

"That's not fair," Binny said. "I want a turn."

"Me too! Me too! Me too!" all of Banoffee's children cried. "Let's get

Renard. Let's get Renard. Let's get Renard!"

"*Caramba!* Are you crazy?" Eduardo yelled. "I said no, OK? No means no."

Coco couldn't help giggling. It was Eduardo's turn to find out how difficult it was to teach Binny how to behave!

Eduardo glared at her. "If that fox turns up, we jump in the burrow where he can't get us," he said. "You understand?"

Binny and the little guinea pigs nodded.

"Good. We will start by foraging. Get into two groups."

The guinea pigs and Binny pushed and shoved while they decided who wanted to be with whom.

"Man, this is hard work!" Eduardo grumbled.

"I told you so!" Coco grinned.

Eduardo sorted the squabbling babies out. "Now listen up! I want you to find everything you can. You never know what will come in useful when you are a freedom fighter! Off you go, but don't go too far."

The two groups rambled off.

Coco and Fuzzy watched as they disappeared into the fringes of the long grass.

Five minutes later the first group—the one without Binny—returned.

"What have you got?" Eduardo asked.

The guinea pigs turned out the contents of Pepper's basket.

There was a bottle top, an elastic band, a box of matches, a piece of chewed chewing gum, a ball of string and some dandelion stalks.

"Excellent!" Eduardo congratulated them.

Just then the other group returned.

"Look what Binny found!" Blossom squeaked.

Binny's tail emerged from the long grass, followed by Binny's bottom and Binny's body. Her legs were straining against the ground, as if she was pulling a heavy weight. Finally her head emerged, with her ears flat. She was dragging something big into the clearing.

The guinea pigs stared at it in awe. It was an old toy truck. A big one—with two doors at the front and a flatbed at the back to put things on.

"Well done, Binny!" Fuzzy scuttled over. He loved mechanical things. He walked around the truck to inspect it. "Looks like it's battery- operated," he said.

"Do you think it will work?" Coco asked.

"There's only one way to find out." Fuzzy opened the door.

"I'll drive." Before anyone had a chance to stop her, Binny hopped in and pressed the start button. The truck fired up.

"No!" Eduardo shouted. "You're not old enough. You could have an accident." He threw himself on to the truck, wriggled through the window beside Binny and switched the engine off.

"Not fair." Binny scowled. "I found it."

"Come on, Binny," Coco pleaded. "Eduardo's right. You're not old enough to drive. Come and see what the others found."

Reluctantly Binny got out of the truck and went over to take a look.

Eduardo and Fuzzy followed. Eduardo turned the items over with a paw.

"Here you have everything you need to survive in the wild," Eduardo said, sounding pleased. "Warmth, food and weapons. First I will show

you how to make a fire." He gathered
a pile of twigs together on a patch
of earth and showed the campers
how to light a match. "It must not
be somewhere where it will cause a
bigger fire," he explained, placing the
match under the twigs. "So keep it
away from the bushes. Next is food."
He picked up a piece of dandelion
stalk and held it out to the flames.

Fuzzy sniffed. "Roasted dandelion
stalk! Delicious!" he said. Fuzzy loved
to cook. He picked up a stalk and
started to roast it too. So did all the
little guinea pigs.

Coco was relieved to see Binny
do the same. She seemed to have
forgotten all about the truck and
was fascinated by what Eduardo was
doing instead.

"Finally, you must be able to defend
yourself," Eduardo said when they had
eaten their dandelion stalks. "These
can be used as weapons." He pointed
to the elastic band,
the bottle top, the
chewing gum,
and the string.

Binny stared hard at them.

"Ooohhh!" said the little guinea piglets.

"Uh-hum!" Coco wasn't sure it was a good idea for Eduardo to teach the little guinea piglets and Binny about weapons. She shook her head at him.

"But you have to be an experienced fighter like me to use such dangerous tools," Eduardo added hastily. "Come, *amigos*, you have had a busy afternoon. Let us rest a while and sing songs around the campfire. Then I will take you home."

"I'm still hungry," Binny said. She started whispering to Blossom.

"Me too!" Blossom started whispering to Pepper.

"So am I!"

Soon all the little guinea pigs were whispering with Binny.

"We're starving," they complained.

Eduardo sighed. "Very well. I, Eduardo Julio Antonio del Monte, will find food for you." He beckoned to Coco and Fuzzy. "Come help me, friends." He pointed in the direction of the fence and winked.

"No thanks," Coco said. "I'm not

much good at foraging."

"I think he means at Banoffee's place," Fuzzy explained in a low voice. "We can go and get their supper and bring it back."

"Oh, I see." Coco got up.

So did Fuzzy. "Do you think we should leave them alone?" he asked in a worried voice.

"Pah!" Eduardo said. "You domestic guinea pigs worry too much. Look at them—they're having a great time! And they have been trained by a professional. Me! They'll be fine."

Binny and the guinea pigs were giggling away.

"I think I'd better stay and keep an eye on them," Fuzzy said.

"We'll only be a minute, Fuzzy," Coco said. "Come on. You deserve a break."

"Maybe you're right," Fuzzy agreed. His stomach was rumbling, and Banoffee's supper was always very good.

"I will give them instructions." Eduardo took charge again. "One of you, keep a look out for Renard!" he ordered. "Any sign of that fox and you all jump straight into the burrow. Anyone want to volunteer?"

"I will," Binny said obediently.

Coco and Fuzzy exchanged glances. Eduardo's camp really seemed to have worked on Binny. She was being so helpful. Maybe she would find an owner after all.

"See?" Eduardo said proudly. "I told you I'd get her licked into shape. No problem. Trust me, *amigos*, nothing will go wrong."

5
Chocolate

Eduardo was right: nothing did go
wrong. Well, not for the first minute
after he, Coco, and Fuzzy left Binny
and the young guinea pigs in the copse.
As soon as they had gone, Binny trotted
over to the old oak, turned around
so that her back was to the tree, then

stood at attention, like a guard outside a palace. Although it was Binny who had volunteered to look out, the other guinea pigs wanted to help so they followed her and did the same. Soon all fourteen little creatures were standing in a ring, around the tree.

No one giggled, or hummed, or

farted. They all looked out across the copse, making sure that they were safe from harm.

Then Blossom saw something on the ground. It was small and round and brown, but it wasn't a coin or a button.

It looked like—but it couldn't be—it wasn't Easter quite yet—but it looked like—yes, it DID look like a piece of CHOCOLATE. She nudged Binny, who was standing next to her.

"Can you see what I see?" she asked, because she was always full of questions.

"What letter does it begin with?" asked Binny, who thought it was a game.

Blossom answered with a nod toward the chocolate. Binny turned her head and saw what Blossom saw. She took a step forward, toward the chocolate. The other guinea pigs did the same. Binny turned back to them and held up her paw.

"Stay there!" she ordered. "Let me see if it's safe."

She crept toward the chocolate. She crouched down and sniffed. Then, when she was sure it was safe, she licked it. And then she ate it up, all in one bite!

The guinea pigs sighed and moaned.

"That's not fair!" cried Pepper.

"Can I have some?" asked Blossom.

Binny put her paw in the air and silenced them again.

"I'm the Easter Bunny. I get to try it first," she explained. "And now you can all have some. Look!"

Binny pointed at the ground in front of her. There, a little way away, was another piece of chocolate!

The guinea pigs were so excited. They all rushed forward. Binny put her paw up again. Everyone stopped and listened.

"Blossom first, because she saw the chocolate first."

The others nodded in agreement. This seemed fair. Blossom came forward like a little girl winning a big prize. As soon as she got to the chocolate she grabbed it and started to nibble at it excitedly. The other guinea pigs cheered. Then Binny pointed out another piece of chocolate. And so it went on, because there was a trail of chocolate stretching ahead, enough for everyone.

The guinea pigs were so busy chomping their chocolate they didn't notice that the trail had led them into the long grass, and from there into the thick bushes. One after another, each guinea pig found their piece of chocolate, until Pepper was the only one who hadn't had any. By the time it was her turn she had reached a rather dark part of the copse. It was under a low tree with big leaves that let in very little light.

She looked around for the chocolate. Where was it? Whoever had left the chocolate must have known that there were fourteen little creatures who all wanted some. It wouldn't be fair to leave anyone out. She began to feel a little scared. She was all alone. Everyone else was busy enjoying their treat. She wondered who had left the chocolate trail. Was it their nice mom, Banoffee? Was it Eduardo, their teacher? Or was it Coco and Fuzzy? Or another guinea pig they didn't know?

Just then Pepper saw something move. It didn't look much like a guinea pig. It had four long legs, orange fur, a long bushy tail and very sharp-looking white teeth.

"The fox!" Pepper exclaimed. "We should have guessed it was him!"

Everyone had forgotten about Renard. But he hadn't forgotten about the guinea pigs and their new little bunny friend. He had been watching and listening all along. And he had laid the trail of chocolates in order to draw them out.

He stepped out from behind the tree.

"What big eyes you've got!" Pepper squeaked.

"All the better to see little guinea pigs with," the fox replied.

"What big ears you've got!" Pepper squealed.

"All the better to hear little guinea pigs munching chocolate," he sneered.

"What big teeth you've got," Pepper whispered.

"Thank you. They're all my own," said the fox proudly. "It's very important to have regular checkups at the dentist, you know. And clean your teeth after every meal. I will be cleaning mine after I've eaten you."

Pepper screamed at the top of her voice.

"No point crying out, my little friend, you'll never escape!" said the fox.

But there *was* a point in crying out. The other guinea piglets immediately stopped eating their chocolate and raced toward the cry as Renard ran off with Pepper in his jaws.

The little guinea pigs chased
after him. Suddenly there was a roar
behind them. Not an animal's roar
but the roar of a truck. It was Binny!

"Quick! Jump in the back!" she
called out. She slowed down and the
guinea piglets jumped in as fast as
they could. Once they were all aboard
they raced through the long grass after
Renard.

"Attack!" instructed Binny, holding
the bottle top out of the truck window.
Blossom reached out and took it.

"What do we do with it?" she asked.

"Stick it to this," Binny said,

holding out the chewing gum. "Then use the elastic band to catapult it at the fox's nose."

Binny handed up the elastic band and the guinea pigs followed her instructions. One held one end of the rubber band; another held the other end.

Blossom stuck the chewing gum to the bottle top, then she pulled back the middle part of the rubber band as far as she could, placed the sticky bottle top in front of it and let go. The bottle top flew through the air. Blossom's aim was perfect. It landed on Renard's nose.

PLINK!

The sharp, pointy bits of the bottle top hit him right on his soft, black snout.

Renard cried out, opening his jaws wide. Pepper dropped out of Renard's mouth to the ground. Binny braked and the truck screeched to a halt. The fox stroked his snout sulkily with his paw.

"Quick, Pepper, climb up!" called Binny.

Pepper spun around and raced away from the fox toward the truck. Binny opened the passenger door and Pepper leaped in. All her brothers and sisters cheered from the back of the truck.

"Give me the string," Binny instructed Pepper.

Pepper picked up the string from the truck floor and handed it to

Binny. Quick as a flash, she tied a
knot to make it into a lasso. Then
she leaned out of the window and
launched the lasso toward the fox.
The loop fell neatly around Renard's
neck. Binny pulled it tight and Renard
crashed to the ground.

"CHARGE!" Binny leaped out of the truck, followed by the guinea pigs. She dashed over to Renard and used the rest of the string to tie his legs together. The fox snarled and snapped but he couldn't get free. The guinea pigs cheered and cheered.

Binny looked up with a grin. "Anyone for roasted fox's tail?"

6
Foxed

"Let me go!" the fox cried.

"No," Binny said. "We're going to roast your tail."

There was a shout from the branches above.

"*Oi!*"

Binny and the guinea piglets

looked up to see what it was.

Something flew through the air on a vine and landed beside the truck.

It was Eduardo.

"*Qué pasa?* What do you think you are doing?" he shouted at Binny.

Binny looked at him in surprise. "I'm doing what you told me," she said. "I'm using the things we found in the copse as weapons."

The fox twisted his neck so he could see Eduardo. "I might have known you were behind this," he snarled. The fox and Eduardo were old enemies.

Eduardo ignored him. "I told you, you have to be an expert in freedom fighting before you take on the  fox," he yelled at the campers. "Whose idea was this anyway?"

Binny blinked at him. "Mine!" she said proudly.

Just then Coco and Fuzzy rushed up. Coco gave a little scream when she saw Renard.

"You as well!" the fox cried. He tried to wriggle free, but the string held him tight.

"Don't worry," Binny said proudly. "I tied him up, like Eduardo told me. We're going to roast his tail. Do you want some?"

"I did not tell you to tie him up!" Eduardo yelled.

"You did tell them about the weapons, though," Coco said.

"So it *was* you!" the fox growled. "I'll get you for this."

Eduardo ignored him. So did Coco.

"But Renard laid a sneaky trail of

chocolate!" Pepper said, coming to
Binny's defense.

"And he tried to eat Pepper!"
Blossom said.

"Did you?" Coco asked Renard.

"Maybe." Renard admitted.

Coco ignored him. So did Eduardo.

"He wouldn't have tried to eat
Pepper if you'd stayed by the burrow
like I told you." Eduardo fumed at
Binny.

"I knew we shouldn't leave them
on their own," Fuzzy sighed. "I think
this is my fault."

"It's not your fault, *amigo*,"

Eduardo said. "It's Bunny the binny's fault."

"You mean Binny the bunny." Coco corrected.

"That's what I said." Eduardo insisted.

"No, it's not."

"Yes, it is."

"No, it's not."

"Er, hello!" the fox called. He was getting fed up with being ignored. "Could someone please let me go so I can start chasing you again?"

"So *we* can start chasing *you*, you mean!" Binny said.

The guinea piglets all started chanting, "Let's roast his tail! Let's roast his tail! Let's roast his tail!"

"That's enough!" Eduardo thundered. He rounded on Binny. "You are a very bad binny," he said. "You could all have been eaten."

"We weren't though," Binny said.

"That's not the point!" Eduardo

shouted. "I told you to stay at the burrow and keep a look out. You are very, very naughty." He began to untie the fox.

"What are you doing that for?" said Binny, astonished.

"Stop asking stupid questions!" Eduardo said. "I need the string to make a hammock!"

Binny's lower lip started to quiver.

Fuzzy and Coco both noticed it. Eduardo being so upset with her had made Binny want to cry.

Coco didn't know what to do. She could understand why Eduardo was upset with Binny. (She had been upset when Binny was naughty in her lesson, too.) But she didn't want Binny to get upset again.

"That's enough, Eduardo," she said. "Binny was doing really well. Don't be so hard on her."

"We'd better get her back to the house," Fuzzy whispered. "Come on, Binny. Let's go check the website. We need to check how many people are coming to help clean up the rescue center."

"All right," said Binny reluctantly.

"Home time!" Coco said brightly.

She gathered all the little guinea piglets together. They crowded into the back of the truck with Binny.

Fuzzy and Coco jumped in the front seat. Fuzzy started the engine. He knew they might need to make a quick getaway if Renard decided to chase them.

Eduardo finished untying the fox and jumped in after them.

The truck roared off through the copse.

"I'll get you!" Renard called, but he didn't chase them because he was tired from being tied up. "Next time . . ."

Soon the guinea pigs and Binny arrived back at the garden fence. The babies tumbled out of the back of the truck with Binny. Eduardo ushered them under the gate to where Banoffee was waiting in the garden.

"Did you have a nice time?" she said.

"It was great!" Blossom squeaked.

"We had chocolate!" Pepper squealed.

"The fox laid a trail," Blossom explained.

"He tried to eat me." Pepper finished.

"And I caught him!" Binny boasted.

"He cleans his teeth twice a day, Mom," Blossom told her. "Pepper said."

"Oh!" Banoffee looked a bit confused. "That's nice."

"What time do the lessons start tomorrow?" Coco asked Eduardo.

"There aren't going to be no lessons." Eduardo scowled.

"But you said you would teach Binny." Coco protested.

"So did you," Eduardo retorted, "and look what happened to that."

Binny's lower lip started to quiver again.

"I want to be a freedom fighter," she said in a small voice, "like Eduardo."

Eduardo was still angry. "You, Bunny," he said sternly, "will never be a freedom fighter. You don't have what it takes."

Binny began to sob.

"Now look what you've done," Coco said angrily.

"Oh dear," Fuzzy said. "Come on, Binny, let's go look at the computer." He put out a paw.

"No!" Binny backed away. "I don't want to go with you. I want to be a freedom fighter."

"Binny . . ." Coco began. She put out a paw too.

Binny took another step away. Binny's feet were big so by this time she was getting quite far away from the guinea pigs.

Eduardo decided to take charge. "Bunny," he commanded, "do as they tell you. You cannot be a freedom fighter."

"Yes, I can," Binny said. She hopped backward.

"No, you can't!" Eduardo said gravely. "You cannot survive alone in the wild."

"I can!" Binny said. She had reached the fence. "Anyway, I don't want to be with any of you. I hate you all. Just like you hate me."

To the guinea pigs' horror she ducked under the fence and disappeared.

7
Capture

"Can we go look for Binny?" asked Blossom, staring out into the copse.

"Can we have supper first?" asked Pepper, looking at the nice picnic that Banoffee had made for their supper.

"I will go look for Bunny," Eduardo

said. "This is work for a professional, like me."

"We'll come too," Fuzzy said.

But just then they all heard a ring. It was Henrietta's bicycle bell. She always rang it to let next door's cat, Alan, know that she was coming, so he would stop sunbathing in the middle of the pavement and move out of her way. He never did move so she always got off her bike and wheeled it carefully past Alan, but she kept hoping that one day he'd get the message.

Fuzzy and Coco froze. Henrietta was home early! They had to get back to the house and into their hutch before she found out they weren't there.

"Run, *amigos!*" Eduardo urged them. "Here, take my skeleton keys so you can join me later in the search for Bunny." Eduardo tossed his satchel to Fuzzy.

Without a word, Fuzzy and Coco scampered off.

"Come along, kids." Banoffee understood that this was an emergency, so she quietly rounded up her babies and took them and the food back to her hutch next door, where they had an indoor picnic.

Coco and Fuzzy just made it into their hutch as Henrietta came downstairs into the kitchen. They even remembered to close the new lock so that she wouldn't realize they had gotten out again. Coco buried Eduardo's satchel under the hay. Then they both shut their eyes and rolled into balls, to make it look as if they had been sleeping all afternoon.

Henrietta checked that Ben's favorite grapes were still on the table. Then she went over to say hello to the animals.

Coco nudged Fuzzy—they had to try to tell Henrietta what happened! They got up.

"Binny's gone . . . !"

"She's in the copse . . . !"

"We've got to find her . . . !"

"Before the fox gets her . . . !"

But all Henrietta heard was "*wheep-wheep-wheep.*" Even though she was a vet she thought this meant the guinea pigs were hungry, so she gave them a bowl of cereal before she went to say hello to Binny.

"Binny," she called. "Binny!"

Just then Ben arrived home.

"I can't find Binny," Henrietta told him.

"Let's try again," Fuzzy whispered to Coco.

"She's outside . . . !"

"In the copse . . . !"

"*Wheep-wheep! Wheep-wheep!*"

Again, Ben and Henrietta didn't understand.

"Let's check outside," Ben suggested, thinking it was his own idea. "Maybe she got out." He fetched the pet carrier and they went out of the back door.

"Phew!" Coco said. "That was hard work. There's nothing more we can do now, except cross our paws."

"Yes, there is," Fuzzy said. "We've got a rescue center to save. Pass me the skeleton keys."

Eduardo was looking for Binny in the copse's bluebell patch when he heard

133

the thudding of giant feet. He quickly
hid behind a bush.

He peeped out. It was Ben and
Henrietta—Fuzzy and Coco's owners!
They must be looking for Binny!
Eduardo breathed a sigh
of relief. As soon
as they found her,
he could get on
with making his
hammock.

Ben and
Henrietta walked
up to the old oak tree. They both
looked carefully at the ground. Then

Ben walked around the tree one way while Henrietta walked around the tree the other way. Soon they had disappeared behind it.

Eduardo heard a rustle from inside the bush.

Suddenly Binny shot across the clearing and disappeared into the long grass.

Caramba! Eduardo muttered. Ben and Henrietta hadn't seen her! He would have to chase her back the other way!

Eduardo left his hiding place and raced after the little rabbit.

Just then Ben and Henrietta stepped out from behind the oak tree.

"An Agouti guinea pig!" Henrietta cried. "In the copse?"

"Let's rescue him!" Ben marched toward Eduardo. "Then we'll have another look for Binny."

Man! Eduardo felt upset. Ben and Henrietta sounded just like Coco—bossy. He didn't want to be rescued! Didn't they know he was a freedom fighter? Then he saw their giant feet striding toward him. Eduardo gulped. Of course they didn't know. And he couldn't tell them!

He ran as fast as he could toward the long grass, but he wasn't as fast as Binny. He felt Ben's hands close around his tummy and lift him into the air.

"*Hombre!* Let go of me! I am Eduardo Julio Antonio del Monte, and I live in freedom!" Eduardo cried, but all Ben and Henrietta heard was "*chutter-chutter.*"

"He's probably scared, all alone in this big copse," said Ben.

"Let's take him home and introduce him to Coco and Fuzzy," said Henrietta.

"*Caramba,* I know them already. They are my *amigos!*" Eduardo shouted, but all Ben and Henrietta heard was "*putt-putt.*"

"On second thoughts, why don't I take him straight to Pets2Go and see if Peggy can find out who he belongs

to, while you keep looking for Binny?"
Ben suggested.

Huh? A *pet shop*?

Eduardo wriggled and squirmed
with all his strength, but there was
nothing he could do as Ben popped
him into the pet carrier and locked
the door.

8
Coco Thinks Fast

Back at number 7 Middleton Crescent, Fuzzy was looking at his website on the computer.

"Coco, this is great! We've got three hundred and fifty-seven clicks!" he said proudly.

"What does that mean?" Coco

positioned the squashy cushion below the table so Fuzzy could jump down.

"It means loads of people are coming to help fix the cages and clean up the rescue center. The Easter Fair can go ahead. And some of them want to know more about Binny. I'm going to post another message."

REMINDER!

Help fix cages and spring clean the rescue center ready for the Easter Fair. Tomorrow 10 till 5! Come and meet Binny the Easter Bunny and adopt an animal.

"There. That should do it."

PLUMP!

Fuzzy landed on the squashy cushion and rolled off.

"Oh, Fuzzy, you are clever at computers!" Coco gave him a hug.

"Thanks," Fuzzy said, blushing.

"We need to find Binny and tell her!" Coco exclaimed.

Just then they heard noises in the garden.

"Quick, Coco, it's Ben and Henrietta!" said Fuzzy.

The two guinea pigs scampered back to the hutch.

"Hide the keys! I'll do the door," said Fuzzy.

CLANG!

Fuzzy pulled the door shut while Coco wriggled under the straw as far as she could with the satchel.

"Here comes Ben," Fuzzy said with relief. "He's got the pet carrier."

"He must have caught Binny," Coco said. "Thank goodness."

The two guinea pigs peeped out of the hutch. Ben was closing the back door carefully behind him with one hand. In the other hand dangled the pet carrier.

"But where's Henrietta?" Coco asked. Fuzzy shrugged. "Maybe she went to give Alan the cat a stroke. It doesn't really matter as long as Binny's all right." He breathed a sigh of relief. "It would have been awful if she missed the Easter Fair when so many people are expecting her. I can't wait to tell her about the website."

Just then they heard a sound that made their blood freeze.

"Help me, *amigos*!"

It was coming from the pet carrier.

Coco shot a horrified look at Fuzzy. "Oh no!" she cried. "It's not Binny. Ben's captured Eduardo instead!"

Ben placed the pet carrier down on the floor beside the guinea pigs' hutch. "I'll go get my car keys," he said, to nobody in particular.

"Car keys?" Coco repeated faintly. "Where's he going?"

Eduardo sat down heavily beside

the door of the pet carrier and poked his nose through the bars. "He is taking me to prison," he sighed sadly.

"Prison?" Fuzzy repeated. "What prison?"

"PetsGo2 Prison," Eduardo said. He slumped down on his back and stared at the ceiling of the carrier in despair.

"Oh no," Fuzzy gasped. "What on earth are we going to do now?" He scratched the crest on his head.

Coco thought hard. Even though Fuzzy was great on the computer, he wasn't always very good at working things out. And Eduardo was too busy feeling sorry for himself to come up with anything sensible. She would have to do the thinking, as usual.

"I know!" she said. "You can

escape. With your skeleton keys."

"My skeleton keys!" Eduardo repeated. "That's it, *señorita!* Quick, *amigos.* Give me my satchel."

"I'll get it." Fuzzy scampered to the pile of hay in the corner of the hutch and burrowed into it.

"Where on earth are those darned car keys?" Ben was still searching and was talking to no one in particular. He started opening and closing drawers.

It was a race between Fuzzy and Ben. Who would find their set of keys first? Coco held her breath. She told herself to keep calm. Ben was always losing his car keys. It usually took him ages to find them. Eduardo had plenty of time to escape.

"Hurry, Fuzzy, my friend!" Eduardo urged.

"I can't find the satchel," Fuzzy complained, flicking bits of their bed into the air with his paws. The hay was dense and tangled. Each stalk seemed to have been twisted in a knot around the next one. "Coco's hidden it."

"You told me to!" Coco protested.

Just then Henrietta came in. "It's no good," the guinea pigs heard her say. "I can't find Binny."

Coco felt her heart beat faster. How were they going to tell Binny about the website if they couldn't find her? And that wasn't the only thing worrying her. Henrietta was much more sensible than Ben: she would almost certainly know where to find the car keys. Fuzzy would have to hurry.

Ben burst into tears. "I hate to think of Binny out there all alone," he wept. "That poor defenseless little bunny."

"Pah!" Eduardo spat. "Poor defenseless little binny? Are you kidding me? You should see what she did to that fox!"

"Yes, but Ben doesn't know that." Coco pointed out. "Hurry up with those keys, Fuzzy."

"I'm trying!" Fuzzy panted from under the straw. He could see the satchel but he couldn't quite reach it. He was fatter than Coco and she could get into parts of the straw he couldn't.

Henrietta handed Ben a tissue. She was not prone to bursting into tears herself but she always kept the tissues handy in case Ben did. "I think I saw her tail disappearing under the old oak tree. I had a poke about with a stick. There seems to be some sort of burrow down there."

"Bunny's in my burrow!" Eduardo howled in anguish. "I have to get back there before she does any damage."

"Quick!" Coco ordered. She was beginning to feel really anxious about Eduardo. If Henrietta thought that Binny was safe, it wouldn't be long before the subject got back to taking Eduardo to the pet shop.

"Got it!" Fuzzy's front paw made contact with the strap of the satchel. He gripped it firmly and began to pull. "Darn it, now I'm stuck!"

Ben blew his nose loudly. "Do you think Binny might have found some other bunny friends?" he sniffed.

"Yes, I do." Henrietta said firmly. "So stop feeling bad about her and get this little kid off to the pet shop instead. Peggy will look after him. That will make you feel better."

Coco saw Henrietta's sensible shoes coming toward the hutch. She saw Henrietta's knees bend and her hand reach toward the pet carrier.

"Fuzzy!" she chattered. "Now!"

"Coming!" he panted.

"But I can't find the car keys." Ben complained.

Henrietta's hand hovered over the handle. "Have you tried your pocket?" she suggested, turning to look at Ben.

"Here!" Fuzzy reached the door of the hutch. He passed the satchel to Coco.

Coco opened it and took out the skeleton keys. She got ready to throw them to Eduardo.

Eduardo held his paw out between

the bars of the pet carrier door.

"Here they are!" Ben took out the car keys from his pocket. "They must have been there the whole time. Silly me."

Henrietta looked down again. Her hand closed on the handle of the pet carrier.

"Throw them, señorita!" Eduardo cried.

Coco thought fast. It was too late to throw the skeleton keys. If Henrietta saw her she would think it was very odd for one guinea pig to be throwing a set of miniature keys to another guinea pig. Worse still, she might take the keys away. If Henrietta did that, then Eduardo would still end up in the pet shop and she and Fuzzy wouldn't be able to get out of their hutch to rescue him!

"No." She sat on the keys instead so that Henrietta couldn't see them.

"Then I am doomed!" The pet carrier rose into the air. "Good-bye, *amigos*. It's been nice knowing you."

Henrietta's sensible shoes followed Ben's sneakers into the hallway and up the stairs.

There was silence in the kitchen.

"Uh-oh," Fuzzy whispered finally.

"Now what?"

Coco put the satchel around her neck.

"We'll fix that lock so we can open it without a key like we did before," she said. "Then first thing tomorrow we'll go to Eduardo's burrow and get Binny." She took a deep breath. "And then we'll go to the pet shop and rescue Eduardo!"

9
The Easter Bunny

"I was naughty because I was sad, and I was sad because I wanted to be a pet, and I was jealous of you because you were pets. I never meant to get you into trouble, and I never meant to get Eduardo sent to the pet shop!"

The next morning, inside Eduardo's burrow under the old oak tree, Coco and Fuzzy listened carefully to Binny.

Ben and Henrietta had been woken up early by a text from Peggy at Pets2Go saying that a large line of volunteers had arrived to fix the cages and help clean up the rescue center. The website had worked! As soon as Ben and Henrietta left the house, Coco and Fuzzy had let themselves out of the hutch with one of Eduardo's skeleton keys and rushed to the copse to find Binny.

Poor Binny had spent a miserable
night on her own in the burrow. She
had been too scared to return to the
house.

"I wasn't scared of the fox,"
she explained. "I was scared that

everyone hated me because I've been
so horrible. I felt just like I did the last
time, when I was left on my own in a
box outside the rescue center."

"It's all right," Fuzzy said. "I was
left on my own too, in an old shed at

the bottom of an overgrown garden. But then Ben found me and now I have a nice home, and so will you. I promise."

"But everyone hates me."

Binny's tears fell onto the ground. Fuzzy carefully dried her face with a large leaf.

"No, they don't," Coco said. "We wouldn't have come to find you if we didn't care about you. And you made friends with Banoffee's children. They're all really worried about you. So were Ben and Henrietta. The only reason they stopped looking for you was because they thought you'd found a rabbit burrow and met some other rabbits. They didn't realize that the burrow was Eduardo's."

Binny's face crumpled.

"Eduardo!" she gulped. "We need to help him. We need to get to the pet shop."

In spite of everything, Fuzzy and Coco smiled at each other.

"We knew you'd want to help, Binny," Fuzzy said. "Besides, you're expected at the Easter Fair."

He told her about all the clicks he'd had on his website.

"You mean all those people want to see *me*?" Binny asked in awe.

"Yes, Binny, they do," Coco said.

"Then I'm going to be the best-behaved Easter Bunny in the whole world." Binny beamed, but then her expression changed. "But how are we going to get there?"

Just then Terry popped his head into the burrow.

"You coming or what?" he demanded. "I just fixed the GPS in the truck."

Fuzzy drove the truck. He knew the way from when Ben used to take him to work so he had someone to talk to during his lunch hour. That was when the rescue center first opened. Now Ben usually had cats, dogs, hedgehogs, and a donkey to talk to while he ate his sandwich.

They drove through the park,

along a footpath, around the back of the supermarket parking lot, and past the old people's home. No one saw them. Finally the truck bumped along the alleyway at the back of the main-street shops.

They pulled up beside some trashcans. A pile of chewed wood was stacked next to them.

"That looks as if it's from the cages that I chewed," Binny said.

"That means the clean-up must have begun," said Coco. "The volunteers must be mending the animal cages!"

Sure enough, when Binny and the guinea pigs crept up the garden at the back of the rescue center they were delighted by what they saw. Peggy, Ben, and Henrietta were carrying the animals through a gate from the pet shop next door and putting them in pens on the grass.

Helpers of all ages were busy decorating the outside of the building with bunting, ready for the Easter Fair. And from inside came the noise of sawing and hammering. There was even a smell of fresh paint.

Other volunteers were busy in the
garden, setting up tables with food
and drinks. There was even a raffle
stall and a place to buy Easter eggs.

Ben came out into the garden to see how things were going. A child ran up to him with a banner.

"Where shall I put this?" he said.

Ben uncurled the banner. His face fell slightly. In large sparkly letters it read:

EASTER BUNNY

"I'm afraid the Easter Bunny isn't coming," Ben said, a little sadly.

"But my dad said it was on the website." The boy sounded disappointed. "I really wanted to see her."

The animals listened intently from behind a big bush.

"OK, Binny," Coco said quietly. "This is it. Go on. Go to Ben."

Binny hesitated for a second, but only for a second. Then she raced toward Ben and leaped into his arms.

"Binny!" Ben cried. "How did you . . . ?" But he didn't have time to finish his sentence because just then the children who had seen Binny started to chant:

"We love Binny! We love Binny!"

Coco squeezed Fuzzy's paw. He squeezed hers back. They didn't need to say anything because they could both see how happy Binny looked. Now everyone was cheering: "We love Binny! We love Binny!"

"Pssst!"

The noise came from near the raffle stall.

"Have you forgotten your old *amigo*?"

"It's Eduardo!" Coco cried.

The guinea pigs scurried toward the raffle. They stopped dead.

"Poor Eduardo!" Fuzzy whispered.

Eduardo was strapped into a
dolly's stroller. He had a baby's
bonnet on his head and—worst of
all—he was wearing a baby's diaper!

He had a terrible
frown on his face.

"He doesn't look
very happy," the
little girl pushing
the stroller said.
"I don't think I
want this one."

"Good," said
Eduardo, although of course the little
girl didn't understand.

He scowled even harder.

"These crazy people think I am a *bebé*!"

"It's not fair to treat an animal like a human baby," Henrietta said briskly to the little girl. "They don't like being dressed up. Please give him back to me."

"Can I have a different one?" the little girl asked.

Henrietta undid the stroller strap, picked up Eduardo, and took off his bonnet and diaper. She put him down into the straw of the guinea-pig pen.

"Quick, Fuzzy, now's our chance," Coco whispered.

While Henrietta patiently explained the rules of pet care to the little girl, whose name was Ruby, Fuzzy dashed over to the enclosure and unlocked it with one of Eduardo's skeleton keys. Eduardo scuttled out.

"FREEDOM!" he called. "Who's coming with me?"

He turned to the other guinea pigs in the pen.

"Who's with me? Who, who, who?"

"No one," Coco said, shutting the door to the enclosure. "Now go wait in the truck."

"But I am needed here!" Eduardo replied. "Look!"

Coco turned to see what he was pointing at. Binny had hopped over to the stroller and climbed into it.

Eduardo started toward it. "I am coming to save you, Bunny the binny."

"I don't want saving," Binny shouted. "I am a baby bunny, and I need looking after."

"Leave her, Eduardo," Fuzzy said.

"Wait and see what happens. Let's see what Ben and Henrietta think."

Ruby couldn't believe her eyes. "Look! Look everyone! It's Binny the Easter Bunny! She's in my stroller!"

She stroked Binny's ears gently.

"Can I keep her, Mom?" Ruby asked.

"It's up to the rescue center," her mom replied.

"Can I?" Ruby asked Ben. "Please?"

"Do you promise you'll look after her like Henrietta has taught you?" he asked seriously.

"Yes," Ruby said solemnly.

"And if you have any problems, you promise you will come to see me right away."

"I will," Ruby said. "I'll take care of her forever, honest, I will."

"Then you can have her," said Ben to Ruby, smiling kindly.

Everyone cheered.

The guinea pigs looked at Binny.
She wriggled her nose happily and
gave them a wave with her paw.

"But . . ." Eduardo began, then he
sighed. "OK," he said, as Fuzzy put
a paw around his shoulder, "I get it.
Not all animals want to be free."

10
Website Wonder

The next day was Easter Sunday and, as usual, Ben and Henrietta had their annual Easter egg hunt in the garden. Ben hid eggs for Henrietta, Henrietta hid eggs for Ben, and they both hid eggs for Coco and Fuzzy, only the guinea-pig eggs weren't made of chocolate. They were egg-shaped, but they were made of chickweed and dandelion, which Coco and Fuzzy loved.

Later, when Peggy came around for supper and Easter cake, Coco and Fuzzy went down to the bottom of the garden to share their eggs with Eduardo. He was waiting for them by the gate.

"Here we are, Eduardo," said Coco. "Try these Easter eggs—they're delicious."

"I told you before, *señorita*, guinea pigs don't eat chocolate."

"It's not chocolate, Eduardo. It's dandelion and chickweed," said Fuzzy.

"OK, I'll try one."

Coco gave him an egg. He ate it in one bite.

"Not bad, not bad," he said. "I need to try twenty more just to be sure I like them."

When Coco and Fuzzy got back to the top of the garden, the humans were talking about the rescue center.

"We couldn't have done it without you, Peggy," said Ben. "Thanks so much for looking after all the animals for us."

"It was no problem, duck." Peggy called everyone duck, except for her pet duck, whom she called Peter. "The Easter Fair brought lots of customers into the shop to buy food and toys for the pets they adopted, so you helped me out too, duck."

"It's good the rescue center and Pets2Go are next door to each other, with my veterinary hospital just down the road," said Henrietta.

"It certainly is," said Peggy. "Ben finds them, I feed them and you keep them happy and healthy."

"Speaking of keeping them happy," said Ben, "I'd love to know if little Binny is OK in her new home."

"Yes! She turned out to be such a sweet bunny," Peggy said, "and so clever of her to find her way from the copse to the rescue center."

"Well, look at this comment," said Henrietta, pointing at the laptop.

From Binny@strawberrypark. Happy Easter to all my friends from a very well-behaved Binny who is very happy in her new home.

"Ah, Ruby must have written that!" said Ben. "How nice!"

"I'm still wondering though," said Henrietta as she picked up Coco for a cuddle, "who set up that website about fixing the cages and the Easter Fair?"

"I know, it's very strange," said Ben, picking up Fuzzy for a cuddle.

They smiled at each other. This was because Henrietta thought Ben had done it and Ben thought Henrietta had done it.

"We may never know, ducks," said Peggy, who wasn't sure what a website was.

"Let's hope they never find out," whispered Fuzzy to Coco.

"I won't tell if you won't," said Coco to Fuzzy, although all the humans heard was a soft, contented *"purr-purr."*

Be Safe Online!

Surfing the internet is lots of fun, but there are some things Coco and Fuzzy want you to remember so that you stay safe online . . .

GUINEA PIGS ONLINE

G is for *Go Away!*
Never chat online with people you don't know. Never reply to messages from people you don't know. Finally, never, ever agree to meet up with someone you have only met online—it could be dangerous!

P is for *Private!*
Never tell anyone your personal information, like where you live, your phone number, or your passwords. It's your private information and that's how it should stay—private.

O is for *Oh Really?*
You really can't trust everything you read on the internet. Check any information you learn online with an adult to make sure it's true—you might be surprised how much false information is out there!

L is for *Let an Adult Know*
Finally, you should always let an adult know about what you're doing on the internet. And if you're worried about something that you've seen or read online, tell a grown-up right away—adults can be really good at explaining things that might seem mysterious to you.

about the authors and illustrator

Jennifer Gray is a lawyer. She lives in central London and Scotland with her husband, four children, and an overfed cat, Henry. Jennifer's other books for children include a comedy series about Atticus Claw, the world's greatest cat burglar.

Amanda Swift has written for several well-established children's TV series, including *My Parents Are Aliens*; she has also written three novels for middle-grade readers: *The Boys' Club, Big Bones,* and *Anna/Bella*. She lives in southeast London, near the Olympic park. Unlike Coco, she hasn't met the queen.

Sarah Horne was born in Stockport, Cheshire, on a snowy November day, and grew up scampering in the fields surrounding Buxton, Derbyshire. She is propelled by a generous dose of slapstick, a love for color and line, a clever story, and a good cup of coffee.

GUINEA PIGS ONLINE

VIKING VICTORY

"HILARIOUS!" Micespace.com

JENNIFER GRAY & AMANDA SWIFT

WITH BONUS ACTIVITIES!

GUINEA PIGS ONLINE..... CHRISTMAS QUEST

JENNIFER GRAY & AMANDA SWIFT

With BONUS ACTIVITIES!

GUINEA PIGS ONLINE

BUNNY TROUBLE

"EGG-CELLENT!" Micespace.com

JENNIFER GRAY & AMANDA SWIFT